Illustrated by Jerrod Maruyama
© 2020 Disney Enterprises, Inc. All rights reserved.

Customer Service: 1-877-277-9441 or customerservice@pikidsmedia.com

Published by PI Kids, an imprint of Phoenix International Publications, Inc.

8501 West Higgins Road   59 Gloucester Place
Chicago, Illinois 60631   London W1U 8JJ

PI Kids is a trademark of Phoenix International Publications, Inc., and is registered in the United States.

www.pikidsmedia.com

ISBN: 978-1-5037-5496-6

Disney Growing UP Stories

Gilbert IS Not Afraid

A STORY ABOUT BRAVERY

pi
kids ®

An imprint of Phoenix International Publications, Inc.

Chicago • London • New York • Hamburg • Mexico City • Sydney

"**Good mooorning, class,**" says Ms. Clarabelle.
"Next week, we're going on a field trip to the **Birch Canyon Nature Center!**"
All the students **cheer**...except Gilbert.

OUR READING ❀ NOOK ❀

I've never been
on a field trip before!
Gilly thinks.

When Gilly gets home from school, he tells his uncle Goofy the news.

"**Gawrsh, Gilly**," says Goofy. "**Field trips are fun!**"

"You're going to see nature exhibits and all kinds of really neat, **creepy, crawly** reptiles! Aren't you excited?"

"Sure…I'm excited," says Gilly, looking scared. "But it might **snow**. Then the trip **will be canceled**."

"Huh?" says Goofy. "You usually look on the bright side of things—where's that good ol' **Gilly cheer**?"

"Maybe I left it in my room!"

says Gilly,
and he runs off.

Goofy is confused.

Gilly is usually **curious** and **excited** about everything.
Could something be scaring him?

Gilly looks **worried** on Wednesday morning.
"Uh-oh," he says, "I lost the field trip permission slip.
Looks like I won't go after all."

"Have no fear," says Goofy. "Ms. Clarabelle
emailed it to me."

"Now, how about some fresh-squeezed juice?"

Gilly's classmates talk about the trip at school.

"We're going to ride the bus!" says May.

Bus? thinks Gilly. *But I ride with Uncle Goofy.*

"We're going to have Ms. Clarabelle's cucumber sandwiches!" says June.

Cucumbers?! thinks Gilly. *But I like Uncle Goofy's* **humongous hoagies**!

Back home, Gilly helps Goofy
with yard work…and plans another
way to miss the trip.

I know! thinks Gilly.
I could **dig**
and **dig**
and **dig,**
until this hole reaches all the way to…

"Gawrsh, Gilly," says Goofy. "That hole is **deep enough**. Is something wrong?"

Gilly gulps. "I'm **afraid** to go on the field trip. What if I get **lost**?"

"Admitting you are afraid is **brave**!" says Goofy. "Now let's work on that **fear**."

splat!

Goofy runs to the bookcase and finds one of his favorite books, Flores Flamingo and the Fantastical Field Trip.

Reading about field trips might help Gilly get over his **fear**.

Goofy and Gilly read together.
**"See how Flores stays close
to the other kids?"** says Goofy.

"She never gets lost," says Gilly.
"I can always find Flores in the picture
because of her **wacky** shirt."

Gilly has an idea. If he wears
bright colors, then his teacher
and classmates will see him as easily
as he sees Flores.

"Can I wear something **bright** on the trip?" asks Gilly.

"You betcha," says Goofy.

"I know just the shirt!"

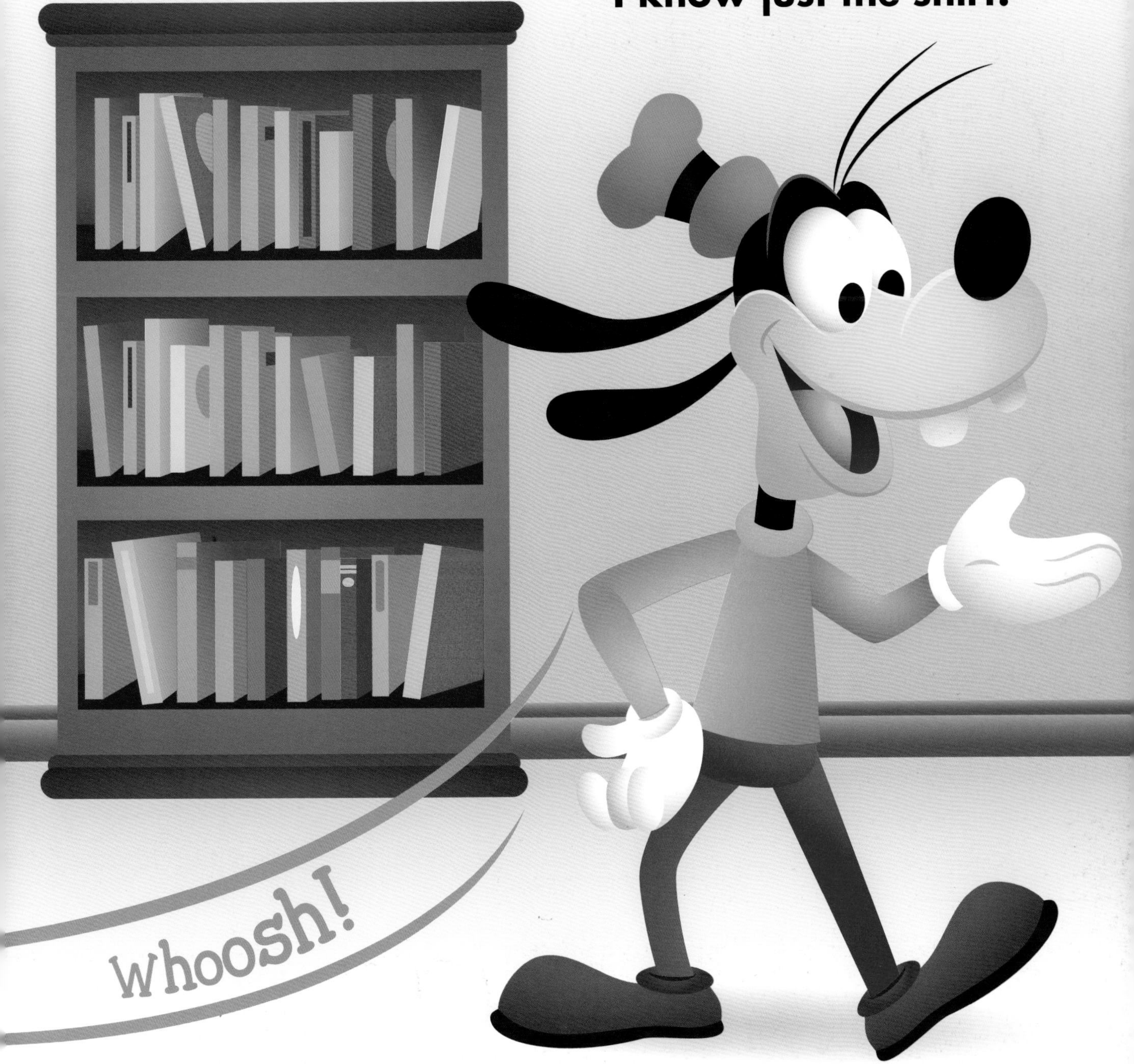

Later, Gilly and Goofy draw
animals that Gilly will see on the trip.

"What if the animals are scary?" asks Gilly.

"The nature center guide knows how to handle them and keep everyone safe," Goofy says. **"Let's hope the little critters aren't too scared of YOU!"**

Gilly laughs. He is feeling braver!

On the morning of the trip, Gilly puts on his **special shirt** and goes outside to the **BIG** yellow **bus**.

Honk honk!

"Let's moooove!" calls Ms. Clarabelle.
Gilly joins his friends and waves goodbye to Goofy.
He is feeling **BRAVE**!

Gilly **loves** the nature center! He is so curious and excited that he forgets he was afraid.

When the guide asks for a brave helper in the **chameleon corral**, Gilly raises his hand.

Hey, thinks Gilly, **I am brave.** I'm even ready to try *cucumber* sandwiches!